MEET THE CHARACTERS

CAPTAIN MARK CHEN
SINGAPORE

A professional soldier, Mark joined the Alliance at age 17. He became the youngest officer ever to lead an Alpha force unit. Protecting an orphanage, he was wounded in combat. Presently, Mark has been commissioned by the I.C.C. to lead a mission to create V.R.E.'s (virtual reality episodes) of the ancient scriptures.

FANTE EGYPT

(Fon-tay) Fante has a quiet, gentle spirit. She is completely deaf, but most eyepiec... readout ... hearing. ... cosmeto... surpasse...

N.A.N.I. MECH HELPER

This prototype mechanical helper was developed in General Hogan's plant. ...ated as a Nureing and ... (N.A.N.I.), she was ...ssist with the domestic ...sion. Her duties include ..., health and hygiene.

YOSI ISRAEL

(Yoh-see) Yosi is an Old Testament scholar. Serious and meticulous in his work, Yosi is considered to be a programming genius. The oldest of the group, among the boys he is the responsible one. He can always be counted on to do the mature thing and act as the "conscience" of the group.

...up in a tough neighborhood in New York City. There, through an inner city youth program, a professional athlete befriended him. His mentor instilled in him a love for two things: God and basketball. A competitive and highly intelligent young man, T.J. is also honest and not afraid to speak his mind.

...ERAL HOGAN

Having served as the Alliance's highest ranking officer for 20 years, General Hogan has retired from active military duty. He is chairman of the I.C.C. (International Christian Coalition) executive committee. His manufacturing plant specializes in developing state of the art military hardware and artificial intelligence. It was he who inspired "the mission."

SAFIYA AFRICA

(Sa-fee-ya) Safiya's name means "pure." She is the oldest child in a family of eight children. Having nurtured many of her siblings, Safiya has a motherly way about her. Mik and Mei Mei often rely on her when NANI is elsewhere. Methodical and thorough. When given a task, she does it one-hundred percent.

LAILANI SOUTH PACIFIC

(Lay-lahn-ee) Lailani never goes anywhere without her smile. She is often under-estimated because of her easy going, laid back nature. What people don't always see is that under that charming exterior lies a brilliant young mind and a computer programming whiz.

GENERAL BAKER

Baker is a "tough as nails" no-nonsense fighting man. He began his long military career as an enlisted man. Having received numerous field commissions, he became an officer. Baker joined the Black Brigade where he met Jon Chen. Baker was there when his friend was lost in battle. Now, General Baker commands the Black Brigade.

NIKOS GREECE

Nikos was recommended for the mission by General Mutiah due to his expertise in VR technologies. He is said to be unbeatable in interactive combat games. Nikos is extremely grateful for the privilege of being on the crew and is eager to do his part to the best of his ability.

IVAN RUSSIA

Ivan joins the mission under protest. His father is a member of the ICC board and requested Ivan's participation. Nicknamed "Ivan the Terrible" by his previous peer group, Ivan has always had problems with relationships and authority figures. Ivan now finds himself confronted with the strict discipline of NANI and the duties of the mission.

GENERAL MUTIAH

High ranking officer in the Alliance, and an ICC member himself, General Mutiah has agreed to handle the military aspects of Captain Chen's mission. Though he is a disciplined Military man, he has a soft spot in his heart for kids. He lost his parents at age 7 and grew up in an orphanage.

ESTER SOUTH AMERICA

(Eh-stare) Ester is a gifted athlete and is always eager to engage in healthy competition. She is competent in virtually all of the self-defense disciplines and was given weapons training by her military father. Unafraid, aggressive, and often reflective, Ester is a natural born leader.

MEI MEI CHINA

(May-May) Mei Mei means "Little Sister" in Chinese. She is joyful, inquisitive, innocent and often emotional. Mei Mei loves animals, especially her country's beloved Panda bears. As one of the youngest in the group, she is treated as the "Little Sister." Mei Mei has no natural enemies. Everyone who meets her, loves her.

THE DIVINER

This Supreme leader of Leviathan is of unknown origin. His militant followers have elevated him to the status of "Deity," attributing supernatural miracles to his divine power. Critics attribute these "miracles" to mere trickery. The Diviner is determined to lead Leviathan into total global domination. He despises religion and democracy and is commited to their demise.

RAJ INDIA

Raj grew up in a poor family where he learned to be very resourceful. He began his computer training at age 7 when he assembled a fully functional XK-39 computer by repairing and putting together discarded parts. Raj is confident that he can fix just about anything and never goes anywhere without his trusty "Calcutter."

MIK AUSTRALIA

Growing up in the outback, Mik developed a keen love for nature. Though the youngest member of the crew, Mik pulls his own weight. He is clever, honest, fun loving and a bit mischievous. Mik often sees things from a completely different perspective and was selected for the mission for this very reason.

FANG SHAW

This Mech/Human of unknown origin is a ruthless leader and undisputed second in command of Leviathan. Virtually impenetrable, the formula for the metal alloy used in Fang Shaw's armor is a closely guarded secret. Fang Shaw carries a deep hatred for Captain Mark Chen and an overpowering desire to destroy him and "The Mission."

The Mission

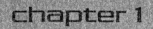

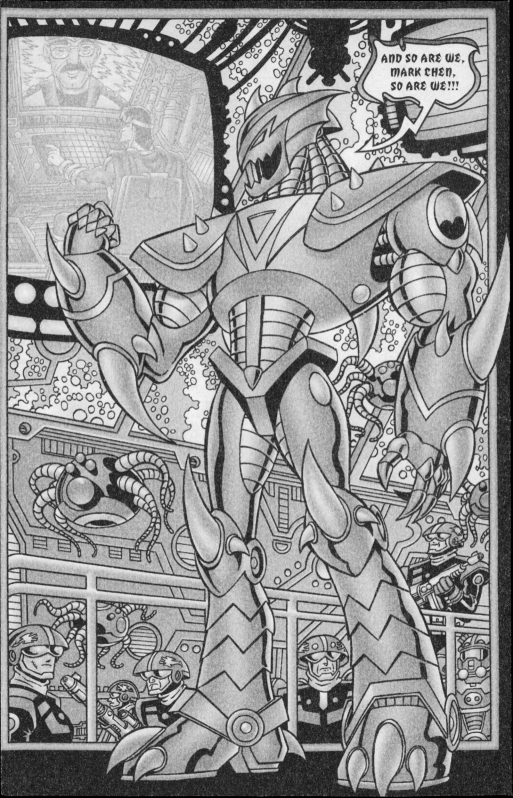

CHAMELEON P-1

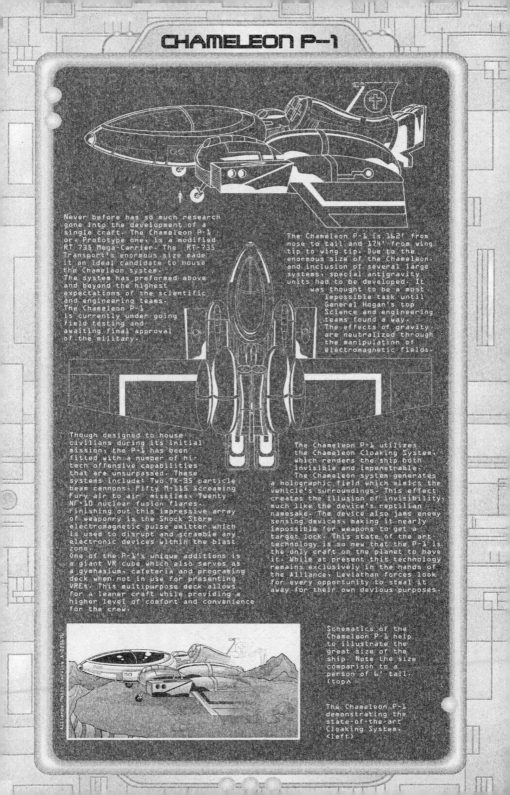

Never before has so much research gone into the development of a single craft. The Chameleon P-1 or, Prototype one, is a modified RT 735 Mega-Carrier. The RT-735 Transport's enormous size made it an ideal candidate to house the Chameleon system.
The system has preformed above and beyond the highest expectations of the scientific and engineering teams.
The Chameleon P-1 is currently under going field testing and awaiting final approval of the military.

The Chameleon P-1 is 162' from nose to tail and 174' from wing tip to wing tip. Due to the enormous size of the Chameleon, and inclusion of several large systems, special antigravity units had to be developed. It was thought to be a most impossible task until General Hogan's top Science and engineering teams found a way. The effects of gravity are neutralized through the manipulation of electromagnetic fields.

Though designed to house civilians during its initial mission, the P-1 has been fitted with a number of hi-tech offensive capabilities that are unsurpassed. These systems include: Two TX-35 particle beam cannons. Fifty M-115 Screaming Fury air to air missiles, Twenty NF-10 nuclear fusion flares. Finishing out this impressive array of weaponry is the Shock Storm electromagnetic pulse emitter which is used to disrupt and scramble any electronic devices within the blast zone.
One of the P-1's unique additions is a giant VR cube which also serves as a gymnasium, cafeteria and programing deck when not in use for presenting VREs. This multipurpose deck allows for a leaner craft while providing a higher level of comfort and convenience for the crew.

The Chameleon P-1 utilizes the Chameleon Cloaking System, which renders the ship both invisible and impenetrable.
The Chameleon system generates a holographic field which mimics the vehicle's surroundings. This effect creates the illusion of invisibility, much like the device's reptilian namesake. The device also jams enemy sensing devices, making it nearly impossible for weapons to get a target lock. This state of the art technology is so new that the P-1 is the only craft on the planet to have it. While at present this technology remains exclusively in the hands of the Alliance, Leviathan forces look for every opportunity to steal it away for their own devious purposes.

Schematics of the Chameleon P-1 help to illustrate the great size of the ship. Note the size comparison to a person of 6' tall. (top∧

The Chameleon P-1 demonstrating the state-of-the-art Cloaking System. <left)

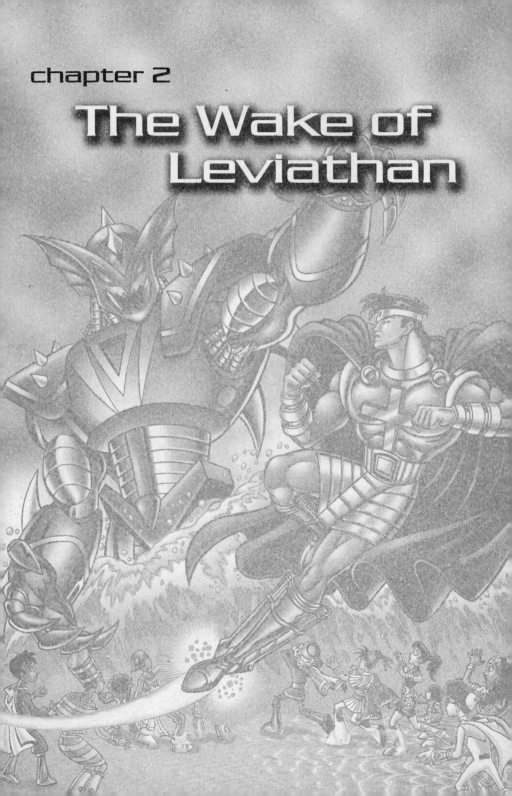

chapter 2

The Wake of Leviathan

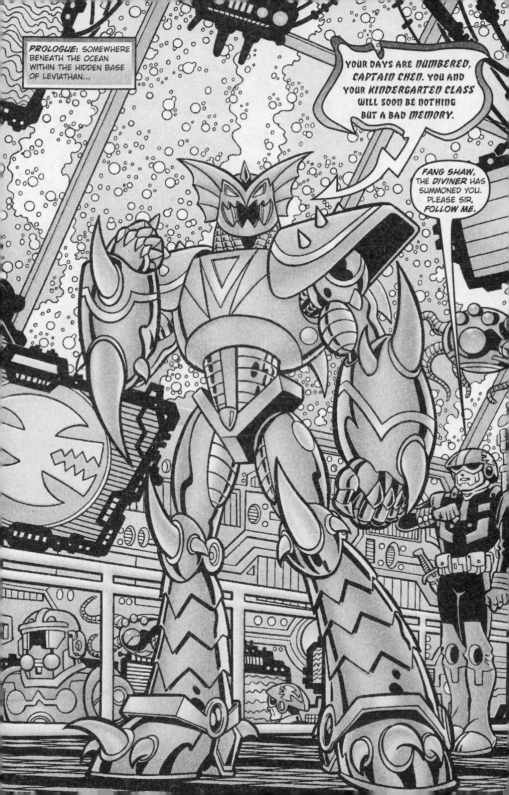

Gen. 6:22 Noah did everything just as God commanded him. -NIV

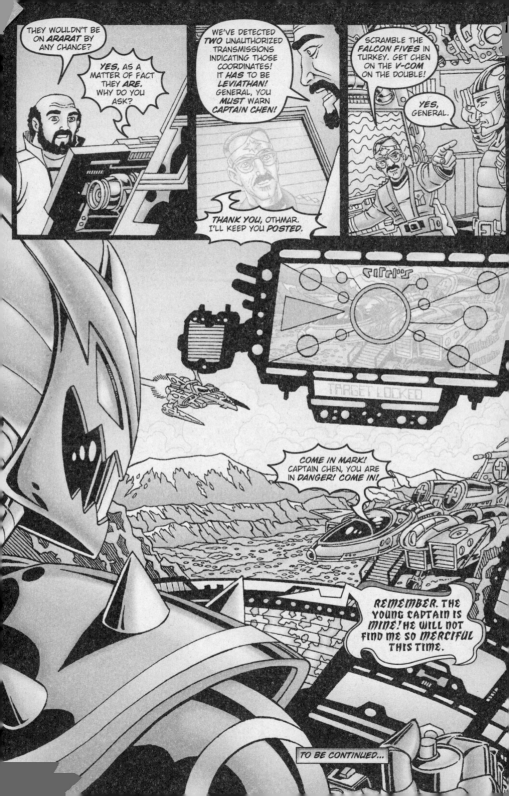

AGE: 14

HOME: A SMALL TOWN ON THE COAST OF A SMALL
ISLAND IN THE SOUTH PACIFIC

FAMILY: MOTHER AND FATHER (LAILANI IS AN
ONLY CHILD)

EYE COLOR: BROWN

HAIR COLOR: BLACK

BIRTHDAY: JULY 3

FAVORITE COLOR: PINK

FAVORITE ANIMAL: DOLPHIN

BEST FRIEND: HALIA, SHE AND LAILANI HAVE
BEEN BEST FRIENDS FOR AS
LONG AS THEY CAN REMEMBER.

PETS: TROPICAL FISH

HOBBIES: SLUMBER PARTIES, SNORKELING,
CREATING VIRTUAL REALITY GAMES
AND STORIES

PERSONALITY: HAPPY AND OUTGOING, LAILANI
SEES THINGS FROM A FRESH POINT
OF VIEW AND OFTEN FINDS
SOLUTIONS TO PROBLEMS OTHERS
HAVE OVERLOOKED. SHE IS A
PEACEMAKER AND ALWAYS
WANTS EVERYONE TO BE HAPPY.

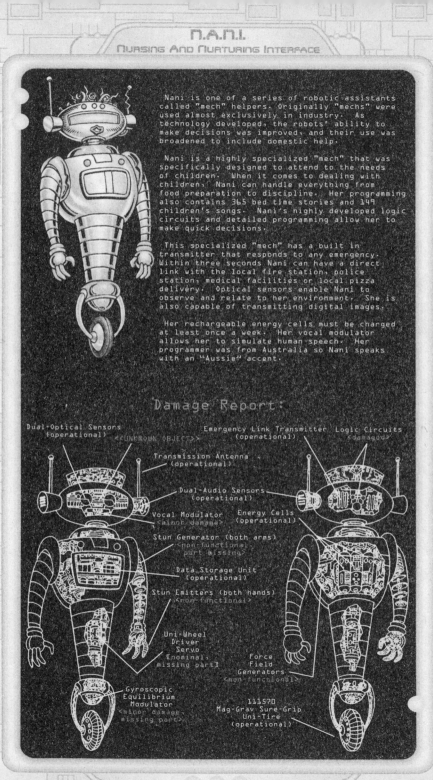

Nani is one of a series of robotic assistants called "mech" helpers. Originally "mechs" were used almost exclusively in industry. As technology developed, the robots' ability to make decisions was improved, and their use was broadened to include domestic help.

Nani is a highly specialized "mech" that was specifically designed to attend to the needs of children. When it comes to dealing with children, Nani can handle everything from food preparation to discipline. Her programming also contains 365 bed time stories and 149 children's songs. Nani's highly developed logic circuits and detailed programming allow her to make quick decisions.

This specialized "mech" has a built in transmitter that responds to any emergency. Within three seconds Nani can have a direct link with the local fire station, police station, medical facilities or local pizza delivery. Optical sensors enable Nani to observe and relate to her environment. She is also capable of transmitting digital images.

Her rechargeable energy cells must be charged at least once a week. Her vocal modulator allows her to simulate human speech. Her programmer was from Australia so Nani speaks with an "Aussie" accent.

Damage Report:

Dual-Optical Sensors
(operational)   <<UNKNOWN OBJECT>>

Emergency Link Transmitter
(operational)

Logic Circuits
<damaged>

Transmission Antenna
(operational)

Dual-Audio Sensors
(operational)

Vocal Modulator
<minor damage>

Energy Cells
(operational)

Stun Generator (both arms)
<non-functional,
part missing>

Data Storage Unit
(operational)

Stun Emitters (both hands)
<non-functional>

Uni-Wheel
Driver
Servo
[nominal,
missing part]

Force
Field
Generators
<non-functional>

Gyroscopic
Equilibrium
Modulator
<minor damage,
missing part>

111570
Mag-Grav Sure-Grip
Uni-Tire
(operational)

GRAVITY BOOTS

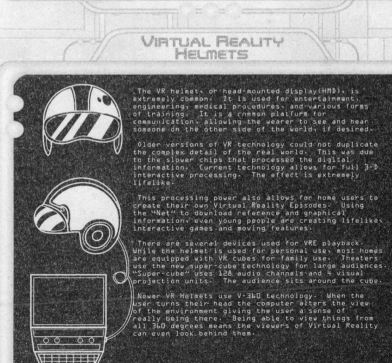

During flight the Chameleon P-1 generates a zero gravity environment. In order to compensate for their weightlessness, the crew wear special "Gravity Boots". "Gravity Boots" utilize two different magnetic fields to simulate the effects of gravity. Without the boots the crew would float around in the ship while it was traveling.

First, the boots use magnetic fields to hold the feet on the floor. The boot holds a positive charge and the floor has a negative charge. The effect is much like a magnet holding to a metal object. If the magnetic force was too strong the crew could not lift their feet. Inside each boot is a microprocessor that monitors the weight and muscular movement of the crew member and then applies just the right amount of charge to allow for a normal "earth" gravity. This allows the crew to go about their normal duties.

Secondly, the boots create an inertial regulation field. While the Chameleon P-1 is in flight it does not always fly in a straight path. It speeds up, turns and stops. At times it is moved about by weather. When the ship bounces around, the boots steady the crew members by creating a force field. It acts like a cushion to keep the crew from being thrown about during bumpy flights.

The boots are lightweight and very comfortable. They contain a special lining called Forma-foam. When a crew member first places their foot in the boot it is very loose. The microprocessor warms the foam. As it warms, it forms a perfect fit for the wearer. The foam is kept at a comfortable temperature and is porous, allowing the foot to breath.

inertial regulation field emitter

forma-foam™

magnetic field generator

micro-processor

contact plates

power cell

contact plates

VIRTUAL REALITY HELMETS

The VR helmet, or head-mounted display(HMD), is extremely common. It is used for entertainment, engineering, medical procedures, and various forms of training. It is a common platform for communication, allowing the wearer to see and hear someone on the other side of the world, if desired.

Older versions of VR technology could not duplicate the complex detail of the real world. This was due to the slower chips that processed the digital information. Current technology allows for full 3-D interactive processing. The effect is extremely lifelike.

This processing power also allows for home users to create their own Virtual Reality Episodes. Using the "Net" to download reference and graphical information, even young people are creating lifelike, interactive games and moving features.

There are several devices used for VRE playback. While the helmet is used for personal use, most homes are equipped with VR cubes for family use. Theaters use the new super-cube technology for large audiences. "Super-cube" uses 128 audio channels and 4 visual projection units. The audience sits around the cube.

Newer VR Helmets use V-360 technology. When the user turns their head the computer alters the view of the environment giving the user a sense of really being there. Being able to view things from all 360 degrees means the viewers of Virtual Reality can even look behind them.

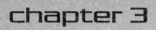

Under Fire

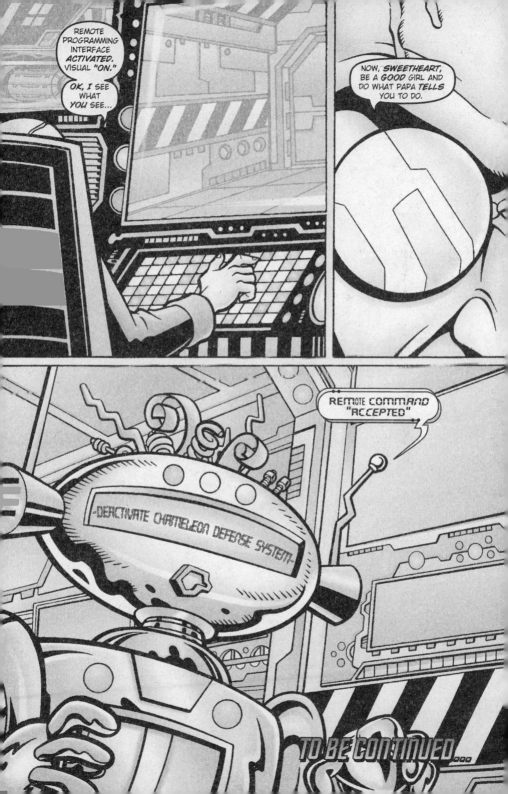

YOSI
IN
THE OTHER SON

Yosi

AGE : 18

HOME : Israel

FAMILY : Mother, Father, Four Brothers

EYE COLOR : Brown

HAIR COLOR : Black

BIRTHDAY : August 31

FAVORITE COLOR : Blue

HOBBIES : Computer programing, studying the Ancient Manuscripts, trivia games, model building and VR programing

PERSONALITY : Serious, meticulous, and Responsible, Yosi is wise beyond his years. His perspective is often that of a scientist/ historian He is meticulous and detail oriented. Yosi is always very organized.

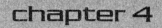

Betrayal

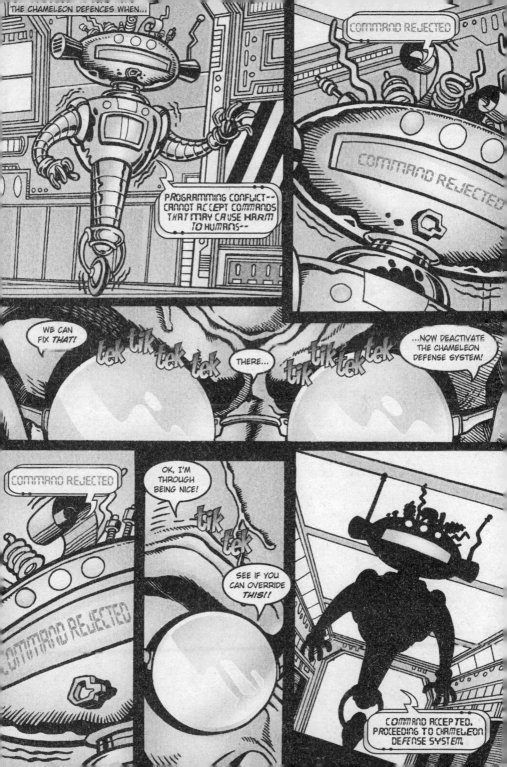

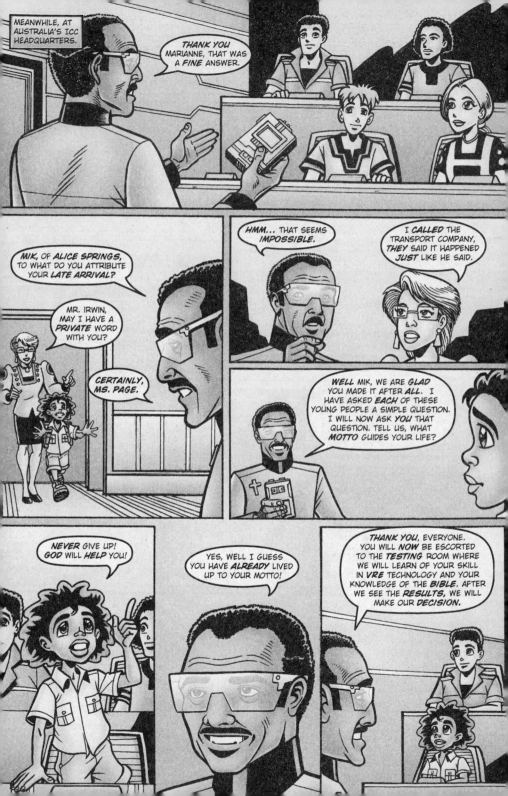

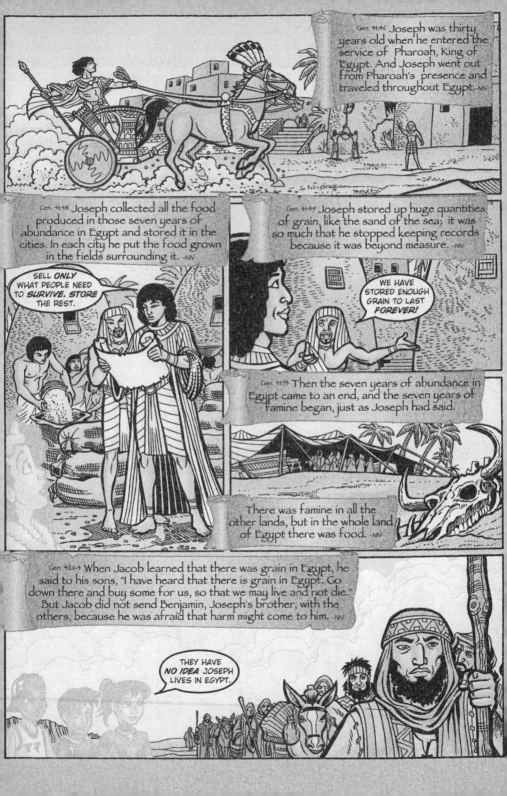

AGE: 8

HOME: A small town in the outback of Australia

FAMILY: Mother and Father (Mik is an only child)

EYE COLOR: Brown

HAIR COLOR: Brown

BIRTHDAY: September 12

FAVORITE COLOR: Red

FAVORITE FOOD: Ice cream

FAVORITE ANIMAL: Kangaroo

PETS: A dog and two geckos

HOBBIES: Loves nature, animals, Exploring the outdoors, Reading Bible stories

PERSONALITY: Clever, honest, fun-loving, determined, adventurous, has a strong trust in God no matter what the situation.

THE NIGHTMARE

Fang Shaw's Ship

Designed to unleash death and destruction, Fang Shaw's specially designed ship is the fastest and most maneuverable fighting craft in Leviathan's fleet. In the air it has been clocked at Mach 12. In water it can cruise at 300 knots.

The wings retract into the sides of the craft while it is underwater. When airborne the wings swing out. Force field generators protect the craft from enemy fire and virtually eliminate drag in the air and in the water, thus allowing for the incredible speed of this fierce vessel.

Two micro fussion reactors power the Nightmare. One powers the engines and one powers the plasma cannons, the life support system and the shields. This merciless craft utilizes electromagnetic lifters for hovering and ground takeoffs.

The Nightmare defends herself with electronic signal jamming devices and anti-missile and torpedo counter measures. The Nightmare's primary weapons are the high yield plasma cannons mounted near the wing hubs. Other attack weapons on board include 200 Shrike missiles and Leviathan's Claw Sensor Lock Torpedoes that lock on target. Also, this beast of destruction has silos for the N-series missiles. These nuclear missiles carry a destruction rating of between one and four. An NX-1 destroys everything within a radius of a quarter of a mile. NX-4 missiles destroy everything within one full mile of the impact site.

Fang Shaw's Deadly Payload.

A Thor's Hammer missile carrying an NX-4 warhead

Carried by the Thor's Hammer air-to-surface missile, the NX-4 warhead would have totally destroyed PowerMark's ship and all inside. Fortunately, Mik was in the right place at the right time.

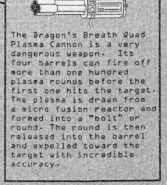

DRAGON'S BREATH
Quad Plasma Cannon

The Dragon's Breath Quad Plasma Cannon is a very dangerous weapon. Its four barrels can fire off more than one hundred plasma rounds before the first one hits the target. The plasma is drawn from a micro fusion reactor and formed into a "bolt" or round. The round is then released into the barrel and expelled toward the target with incredible accuracy.

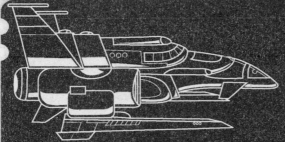

In its' continuing war for total world domination, Leviathan must develop newer and more advanced weapons to aid them in their insidious plots. The Fury A-2 is one of the best of these weapons.

The Fury is a Multi-Environment Fighter, or MEF. It has been designed to fight in the air and sea . The engines are powered by a micro-fusion reactor dubbed the Heart of Fury. The reactor creates plasma for thrust. Since the plasma needs no oxygen, the ship can move freely through outer space as well as underwater. The speed of the craft underwater is 87+ knots (100+ MPH). The ship, while under water, can manipulate its force fields into a shape that allows it to move faster than ever imagined before. The ship is aided in flight by anti-gravity lifters which greatly increase the maneuvering speeds of the vessel. The Fury gives new meaning to the term "turn on a dime". The Fury's top air speed is Mach 7, making it a formidable fighter craft indeed.

The Fury uses a variety of formidable weapon systems. One of the newest is the concentrated plasma cannon system, which draws the plasma from the Heart of Fury. The plasma is drawn into the cannon's ready chamber, then it is blasted out of an emitter. The plasma blasts resemble elongated spheres and may be increased or decreased in intensity. The ship can also carry different types of missiles and torpedoes. There are two types of these that are standard, the Shrike air to air missile and the Leviathan's Claw Torpedo. The Shrike missile is a fairly small but deadly missile. It gets its name from the tiny bird known for impaling its prey on thorns or barbs. The missiles are launched in multiples and destroy by sheer numbers. The second projectile, the Leviathan's Claw, is a torpedo that locates enemy sensors, locks onto the signals and follows them to the source, damaging the target craft.

The Alliance has been ever diligent in its battle against Leviathan. Will this be the weapon that finally leads to the destruction of the Alliance? Only time will tell.

Crew: 1 (Pilot)

Engine: micro-fussion reactor

Thrust: twin plasma thrusters

Air Speed: Mach 7

Water Speed: 87+ knots (100+ MPH)

Defenses: standard force fields, transmission disrupters, missile and torpedo countermeasures

Armaments: two forward mounted twin concentrated plasma cannons,
30 Shrike air to air missiles
0A Thor's Hammer air to ground missiles
08 Dominator air to air missiles
04 Leviathan's Claw Sensor Lock Torpedoes

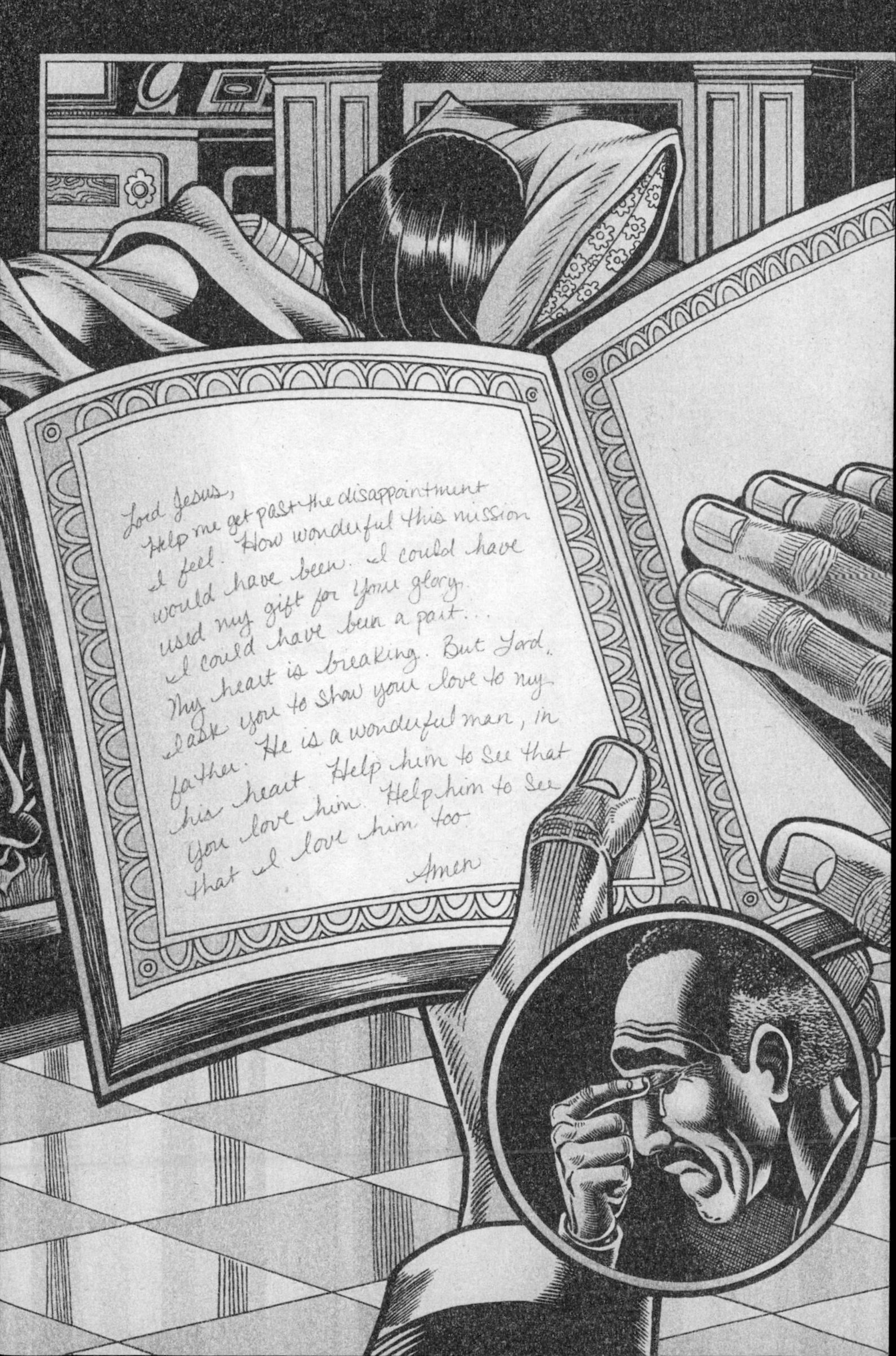
Lord Jesus,
Help me get past the disappointment
I feel. How wonderful this mission
would have been. I could have
used my gift for Your glory.
I could have been a part...
My heart is breaking. But Lord,
I ask you to show you love to my
father. He is a wonderful man, in
his heart. Help him to See that
You love him. Help him to See
that I love him too.
Amen

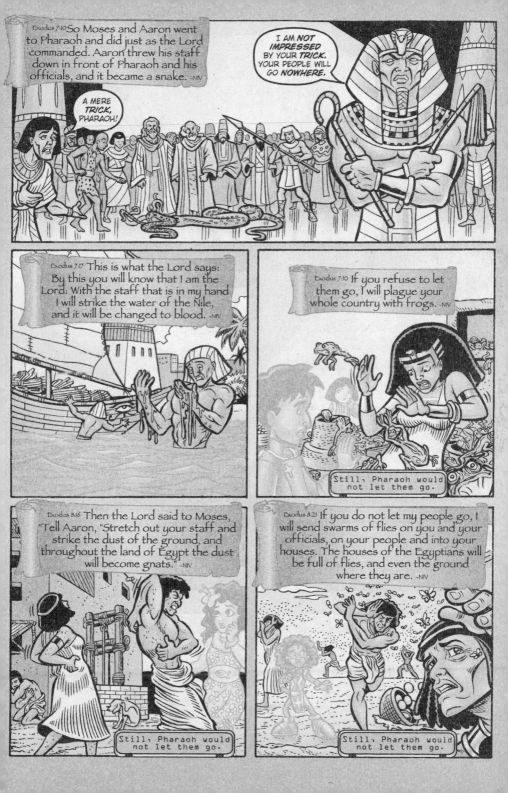

AGE: 16

HOME: A Mansion in Alexandria, Egypt

FAMILY: Mother and Father (Fante is an only child)

EYE COLOR: Brown

HAIR COLOR: Black

BIRTHDAY: February 6

FAVORITE COLOR: Teal

PET: An Egyptian Mau cat named Isis

WANTS TO BE WHEN GROWN UP: A fashion designer

HOBBIES: Fante creates art in the form of holographic cubes and has won several art awards. She also has developed a 3-D fashion design program. She loves health food, shopping, cosmetology and visiting art museums.

PERSONALITY: Quiet, caring, gives wise advice, brilliant mind; Fante is completely deaf, and wears an eyepiece or glasses which give a constant readout of what is going on around her.

Hearing Eye

The "Audio Viewer" nicknamed the "hearing eye" has helped millions of hearing impaired people to experience their world in a deeper way.

Fante has many of these devices, but the one she is wearing on the mission is specially designed to retract when not needed. The eyepiece is connected to a micro computer contained within the headband of her hat. This battery operated micro computer has twelve sensors which pick up sounds all around her.

Various filtering systems are programmed into the computer that can delete sounds or conversations that Fante does not wish to read. Sensitivity controls allow her to hear even the slightest whisper.

The "Hearing Eye" can interpret all modern languages enabling Fante to serve as an interpreter. This amazing technology also allows Fante to focus her hearing. She can focus on one individual sound or on all ambient sound. She can also focus the eyepiece for long distance listening allowing her to read sounds from up to 2 miles away.

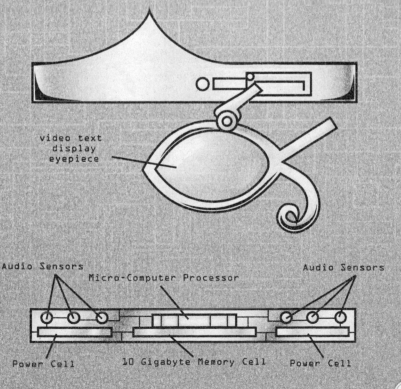

video text display eyepiece

Audio Sensors
Micro-Computer Processor
Audio Sensors

Power Cell
10 Gigabyte Memory Cell
Power Cell

The Black Brigade

Formed during the early days of the Alliance, The Black Brigade is the ultimate special forces fighting unit. Alliance Troops from the Army, Navy, Aerospace Force and Marines are hand picked to make up this elite unit. On land, in the air or space and the sea, this group specializes in high risk, covert operations in any environment. Black Brigade Troops have been conditioned to withstand any interrogation tactic, including torture, without giving up their secrets. However, no Brigade member has ever been captured.

A special team of Black Brigade soldiers has been placed aboard the Chameleon P-1 with orders to protect PowerMark and the Crew from the sinister Fang Shaw and Leviathan. The team has been placed under the command of Major General Gideon Baker for this special duty. Baker normally commands The Baker's Dozen but it was felt that his special talents were needed for this important task.

The Baker's Dozen

The Baker's Dozen Insignia Patch

With the increase of Leviathan's influence throughout the world, it was decided by Alliance command that there needed to be an emergency response team formed to be engaged in the most dangerous of missions. Leviathan would strike quickly. The Alliance needed an immediate response. Under the command of Major General Gideon Baker, twelve Black Brigade troopers were selected. The twelve were chosen for their given specialties and were then put through rigorous advanced training to form the ultimate fighting force: The Baker's Dozen.

General Baker hand picks his personnel. Their term of service is indefinite. Only when a trooper retires or is killed in combat is a new recruit invited to to replace them. They have a saying in the Dozen, "There are only two tickets out of Baker's Dozen, you either retire a hero or you buy the farm." Baker lost a man in combat. Now a replacement must be found. While replacements are normally selected from the Black Brigade, exceptions have been made for those uniquely qualified soldiers. Baker has made his choice, he wants Captain Mark Chen, PowerMark.

EX-L JET PROPULSION BOOTS

Personal Jet Propulsion or PJP devices have been available for decades. Backpack units brought mobility but were large, cumbersome and difficult to control. Due to the position of the thrusters, these units were also dangerous. A replacement was needed. With the advent of Neural Control Technology, as well as Micro Propulsion Systems, a more practical device has been developed. PowerMark wears EXperimentaL Jet Propulsion Boots, which receive commands directly from a microchip installed in his headband. A special belt is used with the unit which generates a protective field around the user during flight. The top speed of the EX-L boots is currently not known, although Mach 1 is considered to be theoretically possible. Developed by General Hogan's plant for use by the military, the EX-L system is a prototype model with only a few units in existence.

Trinesium Chamber

Reaction Chamber

Plasma Ducts

Thruster

VIRTUAL REALITY EPISODE
P-700 ULTRA CUBE

VRE or Virtual Reality Episode is a computer generated program that tells a story using 3-D holograms. After programing VREs are viewed in a variety of ways, ranging from the basic VR headsets to more sophisticated VRE cubes commonly used in most homes. This VRE technology dominates the entertainment industry.

The VRE P-700 Ultra Cube provides the ultimate VR experience. Viewers enjoy a true to life interactive VRE experience. Due to the sheer power of the P-700's computers images appear in high resolution at full life size and in stunning realistic color.

This prototype was designed and built by General Hogan's most experienced Techs for this mission.

The grid section on the floor of the VRE deck is made up of many long cubes that can be raised separately to form any sort of ground work, from natural terrain, to man-made structures. (ie. hills or stairs) People are hologram projections that the people viewing a VRE simply pass through.

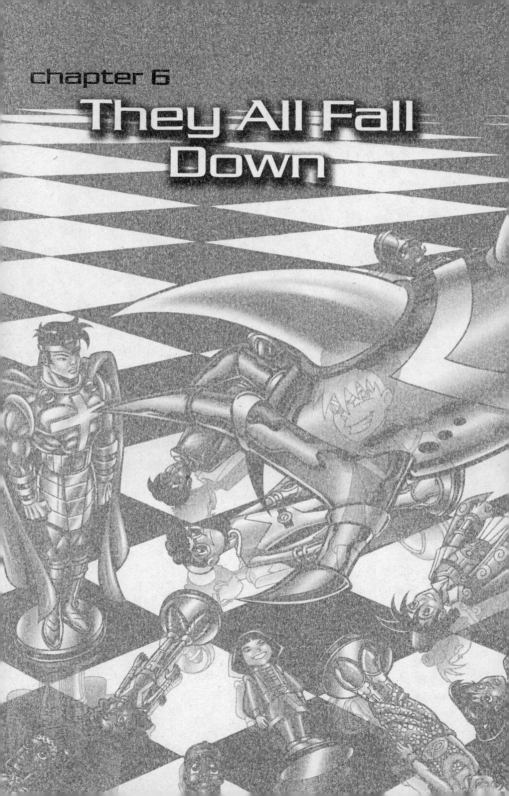

chapter 6
They All Fall Down

POWER

FROM THE FUTURE COME

CAPTAIN
MARK CHEN
SINGAPORE

LAILANI
SOUTH PACIFIC

MIK
AUSTRALIA

YOSI
ISRAEL

FANTE
EGYPT

SAFIYA
AFRICA

MARK

ES OF TRUTH AND PROMISE

Samson
Judges

David
1 & 2 Samuel

Esther
Esther

Paul
Acts

Peter
Matthew

Adam & Eve
Genesis

WILL POWERMARK SURVIVE
THE SERPENT'S TONGUE?
FIND OUT IN...
"operation ascent"
PowerMark: Series 2
ON SALE NOW!
AT YOUR LOCAL BOOKSTORE
OR ONLINE AT: WWW.POWERMARKCOMICS.COM

SAFIYA

AGE: 18

HOME: A village on the savannas of Africa

FAMILY: Father (an important political figure)
seven younger brothers and sisters

EYE COLOR: Brown

HAIR COLOR: Dark Brown

BIRTHDAY: July 10

FAVORITE COLOR: Earth tones

CAREER PLANS: Writer of Children's
Books

HOBBIES: Reading and Writing, telling
stories to her young siblings,
teaching Sunday School, writes
a Christian Teen Viewpoint
column for an Internet news site

PERSONALITY: Responsible and Motherly,
loves children, very
unselfish

Battle Cyborgs

While the Alliance nations outlawed cyborgs, Leviathan, continued to experiment and develop cybernetic robotic machines. Many of their earliest attempts failed miserably, and were discarded. Some, like those who joined forces with Fang Shaw, banded together for their own protection. Programming on these cyborgs was often incomplete, leaving the cyborgs dependent on each other. Alone they are incomplete, but together they believe they can become worthy adversaries.

Left alone for years, these machines began upgrading themselves to complete their programming. Yet, programmed originally for combat, their existence had no meaning, that is, until the day that Fang Shaw arrived at CyborgCity. With the arrival of Fang Shaw and his mission of destruction, they found a sense of purpose.

Shown here is "Mikey." He was originally designed to perform two primary functions. He was built to repair other cyborgs and to serve as an advanced scout. His onboard equipment includes a pair of Infared Capture Units, which are integrated into his optical sensors. This allows him to see in the dark and detect heat coming from humans or machines.

In addition, Mikey is equipped with a special transmitter allowing him to transmit visual information to a remote monitor. Mikey can also recharge batteries using solar power and interface with fiber-optic communications of all types.

Mikey's face is actually a holographic projection that resembles his creator.

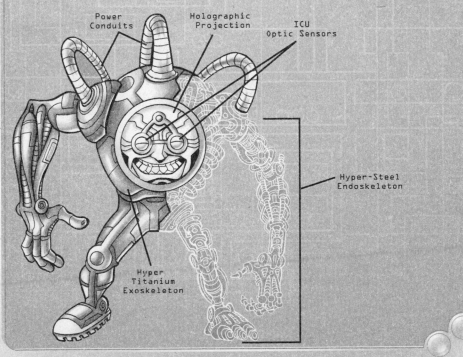

Power Conduits

Holographic Projection

ICU Optic Sensors

Hyper-Steel Endoskeleton

Hyper Titanium Exoskeleton

M·A·R·V·I·N·
Motorized All-terrain Roving VRE Input uNit

The rover (also known as MARVIN) is an excellent all terrain vehicle that can navigate any habitat. Desert sand, steep rocky ground, even mud can't slow MARVIN down. This incredible machine allows the PowerMark Crew access to all the ancient sites, no matter how remote they might be.

With its twin, state-of-the-art quad 360° 3-D hologram-cameras located at the nose of the boom, it records incredibly detailed 3-D images. The smallest details are recorded with amazing clarity. The simulated reality created by this technology is virtually indistinguishable from real life.

MARVIN is used primarily for wide/landscape shots. Its spacious cabin can hold the driver, three additional crew members and cargo. Seated comfortably in the booms control booth, the programmer records the actual site of the ancient scriptures to be used for the background. People and other moving components are programmed into the setting later on the programming deck aboard the Chameleon. This twofold approach to programming brings an unparalleled authenticity to the look and feel of the VRE.

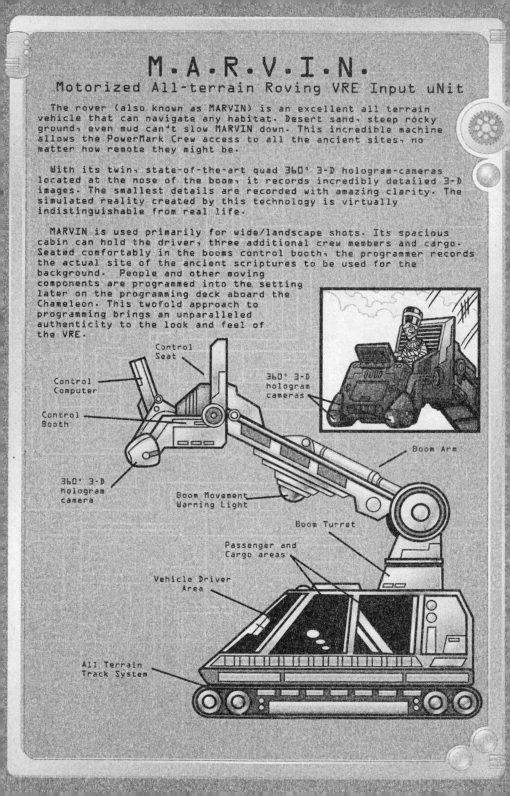

Control Seat

Control Computer

Control Booth

360° 3-D hologram cameras

360° 3-D hologram camera

Boom Movement Warning Light

Boom Arm

Boom Turret

Passenger and Cargo areas

Vehicle Driver Area

All Terrain Track System

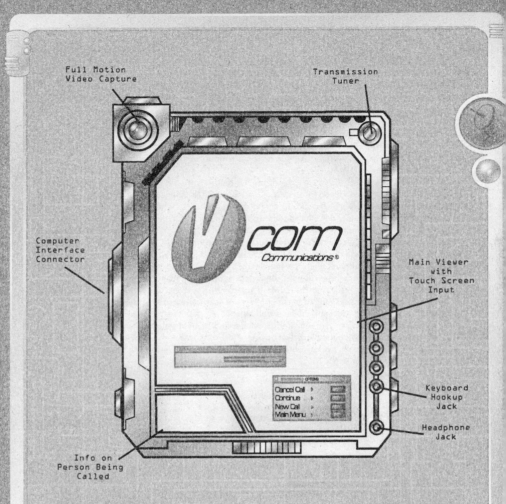

Full Motion
Video Capture

Transmission
Tuner

Computer
Interface
Connector

Main Viewer
with
Touch Screen
Input

Keyboard
Hookup
Jack

Headphone
Jack

Info on
Person Being
Called

OPTIONS
Cancel Call
Continue
New Call
Main Menu

   The V-Com, or Visual Communicator has become indispensable
in PowerMark's world. People from every walk of life use it
to communicate across the miles. These units have an advanced
form of call blocking allowing users to eliminate unwanted
calls. Also, even the civilian units have the ability to
scramble the signal, ensuring privacy.

V-Com units come in a variety of shapes and sizes. They range
from large wall units to much smaller head visors (see next
issue). Hand held units like the one Safiya carries allow for
complete mobility. The unit shown above is referred to as a
desktop or notebook V-Com. This particular unit is the most
popular size made. It is freestanding and can be carried
anywhere. This is the unit the poacher carried when he took
Safiya hostage.

The Alliance combat pilots are known as "Knights of the Sky". They are revered, as pilots have been for centuries, as noble, winged warriors. These pilots share an unspoken code of honor. Skilled pilots are respected even by their enemies. Fighting Falcons pilots are the best of the best. Only the most skilled in combat, the most honorable pilots, fly the "falcon five's" for the Alliance forces. These pilots never leave one of their own in trouble. They will stay and fight until the end. Their motto:. "Together we fly, together we die, but not today."

Under the command of Major General Geoffrey "Jeff" Maddox, the Falcon Five pilots must pass the ultimate test. "Falcon's wing" is the most comprehensive aviation proving ground on the planet. Pilots are put through the most rigorous training regimen in aviation history. Only the best earn the Falcon's wing.

The pilot's gear is state-of-the-art in it's design. The helmet's shell is of a new polymer under girded with a recently developed mesh called Ultra-Grid. Ultra-Grid is created by the interweaving of a newly developed wire which is extremely light weight but extremely durable. The mesh is then molded to the right shape and is embedded into the helmet's outer shell of a hyper durable plastic, making the helmet virtually indestructible. The helmet also has the ability to project the heads up display in the visor. This displays the target and provides information, maps and charts. All this information is supplied via the air craft's main computer and the small computer worn by the pilot. In the event that the pilot must abandon the air craft, the main computer uploads all its information to the pilot's microcomputer and then self-destructs to prevent it from falling into enemy hands.

The flight suit of a pilot has an internal cooling and heating system. The suit also helps the pilot to deal with G-forces and is pressurized In case of loss of cockpit pressure. Under this flight suit the pilot wears a tight fitting body suit which is flame proof. The pilots are also given standard survival gear including a 10mm pistol, survival knife, canteen and first aid pouch.

The Fighting Falcons have been placed on Special Alert Duty under the temporary command of General Mutiah. The Falcons are currently assigned to protect the crew of the Chameleon P-1 at all times and at any cost.

Falcon Five Pilot
In Standard Flight Gear
(wearing pressurized flight/g-suit)

Mini-Computer

Fire Proof Hood

Ultra-Grid High Velocity Crash Helmet

Bullet Proof Visor
(with heads up display)

Oxygen Hookup

Oxygen Regulator

First Aid Pouch

Ultra-Grid Flight Gloves

Survival Kit

"Indestructible" Canteen

10 mm Semi-Automatic Pistol

Secondary Parachute

Holster

Ammo Pouch

Cy-Bar Survival Knife

Ultra-Grid Flight Boots

Collapsible Force Shield

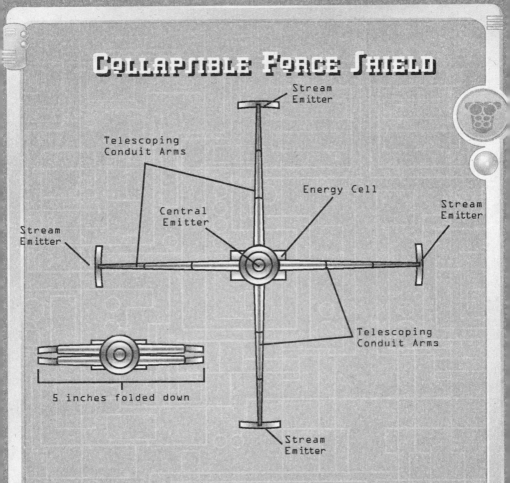

Stream Emitter

Telescoping Conduit Arms

Central Emitter

Energy Cell

Stream Emitter

Stream Emitter

Telescoping Conduit Arms

5 inches folded down

Stream Emitter

This incredible shield was developed by Uncle Albert's security team, Tiger Claw. During the battle with the cyborgs, PowerMark used it successfully to defend against Fang Shaw's particle beam. The Shield itself is made up of energy generated by a series of micro power cells.

The energy is conducted through a hub and four telescoping conduit arms. At the end of these arms are emitters that focus the energy around the perimeter of the shield. The central hub emits energy out toward the perimeter where it synchronizes with the outer field to become one solid shield.

chapter 7

High & Mighty

LATER THAT DAY...

GUYS, NIKOS IS DONE WITH HIS VRE! *COME ON!*

I WILL GET THE *REST!*

OK, NIKOS! SHOW US THE STORY OF SAMSON!

Judges 13:1 Again the Israelites did evil in the eyes of the Lord, so the Lord delivered them into the hands of the Philistines for forty years. -NIV

Then God raised up a man among the Israelites to begin the deliverance of his people. His parents took a Nazarite vow setting him apart to God from birth. No razor was to be used on his head. God's chosen man was Samson.

There was a woman among the Israelites who was unable to have any children.

Judges 13:3 The angel of the Lord appeared to her and said, "You are sterile and childless, but you are going to conceive and have a son." -NIV

Judges 13:24 The woman gave birth to a boy and named him Samson. He grew and the Lord blessed him. -NIV

HE IS BEING WITH *GIANT SIZE MUSCLES!*

GO SAMSON!

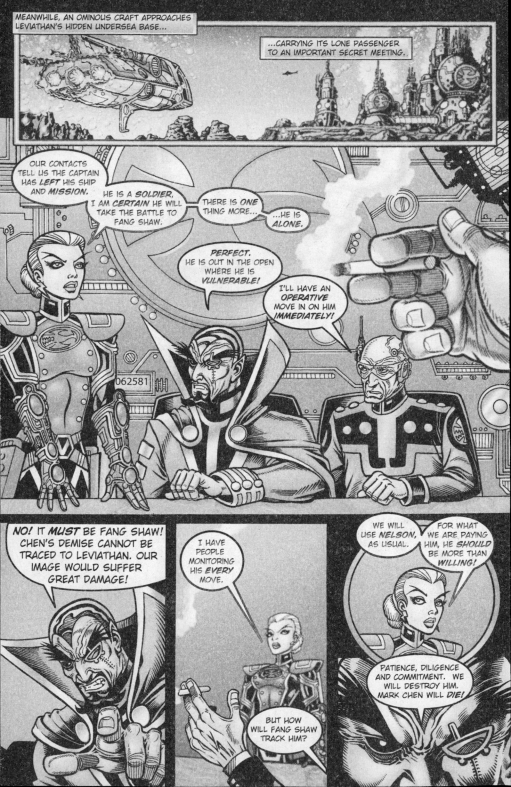

NIKOS

AGE: 14

HOME: An orphanage in Athens, Greece

FAMILY: All deceased

EYE COLOR: Brown

HAIR COLOR: Black

BIRTHDAY: March 17

FAVORITE COLOR: Blue

WANTS TO BE WHEN GROWN UP: Computer Game Programmer

HOBBIES: Computer Games, Fishing

PERSONALITY: Smart, brave, a problem solver, tenderhearted, always stands up for what is right. Nikos' Grandfather, a fisherman, raised him until he was 9 years old. His Grandfather then passed away and Nikos has lived in the orphanage ever since.

chapter 8
Family Matters

AGE: 8

HOME: Beijing, China

FAMILY: Mother and Father (Mei Mei is an only child)

EYE COLOR: Brown

HAIR COLOR: Black

BIRTHDAY: June 12

FAVORITE COLOR: Red

FAVORITE ANIMAL: Panda

PETS: 2 birds

WANTS TO BE WHEN GROWN UP: A veterinarian

HOBBIES: Computer Programming, Mei Mei's father is a Programmer and began teaching Mei Mei basic programming at age 3. She also loves animals, visiting the zoo, and cooking.

PERSONALITY: Joyful, inquisitive, gets along well with everyone. Tells everyone she meets about Jesus.

PowerMark's
V-Com Visor

V-Com or Visual Communicator technology enables remote visual contact even over long distances. PowerMark's V-Com visor is designed for military use. Though it appears to be fragile, its rugged

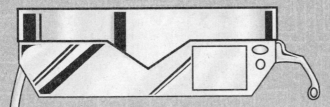

design and construction are able to withstand the rigors of any battlefield. The visor links to a floating V-Sphere camera for two-way communication. This powerful heads-up display unit is also equipped with computer display capabilities, so the wearer can view text or images without distorting his or her normal view. PowerMark's V-Com signals are scrambled using one of the most sophisticated encryption technologies in existence.

PowerMark's
V-Sphere

The V-Sphere is a mobile camera unit designed to track on the V-Com visor automatically. This collapsible unit fills with helium and other gases on deployment. A small anti-grav gyro motor enables it to hover and follow the visor without disruption. As it collects information from the transmitter, it processes the information using its on board micro-processing unit. This information instructs the sphere to move and adjust its position. These constant adjustments provide the best possible visual.

This powerful combination of visor and sphere enables the wearer to transmit visual information across the planet even when he or she is on the move.

TIGER CLAW

虎　虎

Tiger Claw, a specialized form of martial arts, is a closely guarded family secret. It was born many centuries ago within the family of Lai. The early Lai family was sought after to guard very rich noble Chinese families. The Lai family spent decades perfecting what is reputed to be the most powerful martial arts style ever. Tiger Claw was so named because of its fluid and deadly catlike movements combined with an intense mastery of numerous weapons. It typically takes ten years of dedicated training to master "Tiger Claw."

Down through the generations, Tiger Claw remained a secret force. As in previous generations, the Lai family continues to be sought out as security for the wealthy. Lai Wang Chi served as the security chief of Albert Chen for many years before he was severely injured during a fierce attack by bandits on Chen's mountain top compound. Now, from his wheelchair, he continues to serve as chief security officer for Chen. Lai's eldest son, Shen, is the chief tactician and technical advisor. Lai's younger children, fraternal twins Jade and Jai Ren, are specialists in combat tactics. Their twin telepathy allows them to battle enemies in perfect harmony. With these "Claw" warriors on the job, word is, you need an army to get into Chen's mountain compound.

Power Gauntlet with Hidden Plasma Blaster

Missile Darts

Electromagnetic "Tractor Beam"

Power Gauntlet with Hidden Electromagnetic Field Darts Plasma Blaster

Electrical Charge

JAI REN

ULTRA GRID TIGER CLAW ARMOR

This high tech armor was designed exclusively for Tiger Claw warriors, Jade and Jai Ren. Composed of the amazing Ultra-Grid mesh (see issue 3, "Falcon Five" page), the armor is nearly indestructible. This armor is not only strong, it also contains many hidden surprises, which are both offensive and defensive weapons.

Jade

In Her Ultra-Grid Tiger Claw Armor

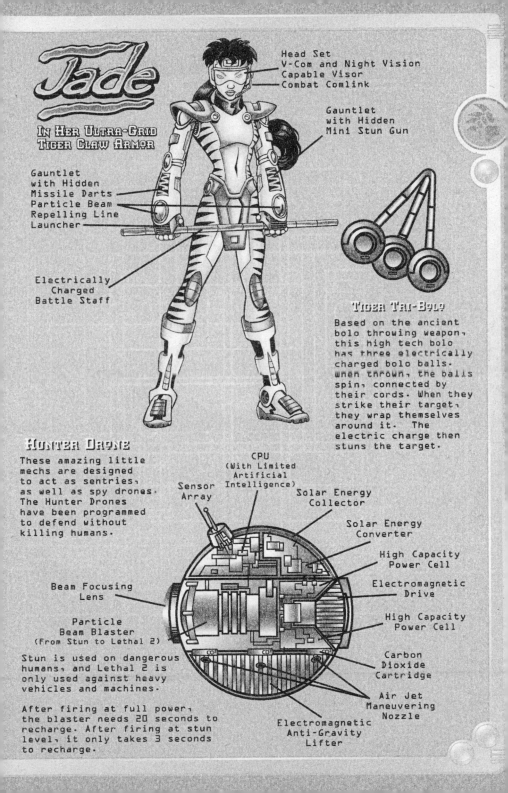

Head Set
V-Com and Night Vision
Capable Visor
Combat Comlink

Gauntlet
with Hidden
Mini Stun Gun

Gauntlet
with Hidden
Missile Darts
Particle Beam
Repelling Line
Launcher

Electrically
Charged
Battle Staff

Tiger Tri-Bolo

Based on the ancient bolo throwing weapon, this high tech bolo has three electrically charged bolo balls. When thrown, the balls spin, connected by their cords. When they strike their target, they wrap themselves around it. The electric charge then stuns the target.

Hunter Drone

These amazing little mechs are designed to act as sentries, as well as spy drones. The Hunter Drones have been programmed to defend without killing humans.

Sensor
Array

CPU
(With Limited
Artificial
Intelligence)

Solar Energy
Collector

Solar Energy
Converter

High Capacity
Power Cell

Electromagnetic
Drive

Beam Focusing
Lens

Particle
Beam Blaster
(From Stun to Lethal 2)

High Capacity
Power Cell

Carbon
Dioxide
Cartridge

Air Jet
Maneuvering
Nozzle

Electromagnetic
Anti-Gravity
Lifter

Stun is used on dangerous humans, and Lethal 2 is only used against heavy vehicles and machines.

After firing at full power, the blaster needs 20 seconds to recharge. After firing at stun level, it only takes 3 seconds to recharge.

chapter 9

Cyborg Mayhem

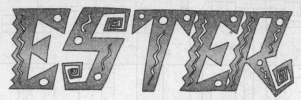

AGE: 17

HOME: South America

FAMILY: Father, two brothers

EYE COLOR: Brown

HAIR COLOR: Black

BIRTHDAY: January 12

FAVORITE COLOR: Green

FUTURE PLANS: Physical Education Teacher/Coach

HOBBIES: Sports, especially Basketball and Soccer, self-defense, coaches kid's sports teams

PERSONALITY: Tough—grew up in a bad neighborhood, smart, outgoing, a good leader, encouraging, loves friendly competition

C/T-3869 CARGO AND TROOP CARRIER

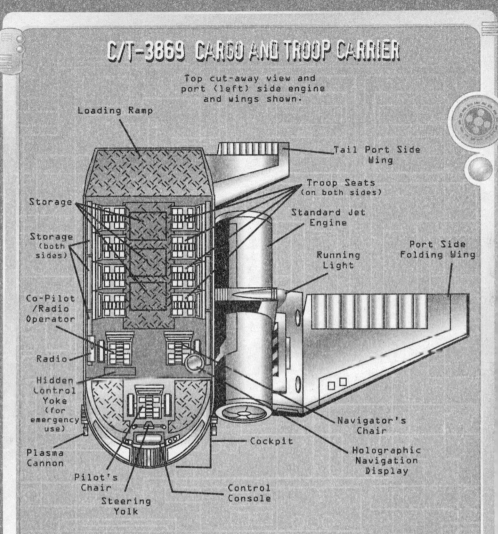

Top cut-away view and
port (left) side engine
and wings shown.

Loading Ramp

Tail Port Side
Wing

Troop Seats
(on both sides)

Storage

Standard Jet
Engine

Storage
(both
sides)

Running
Light

Port Side
Folding Wing

Co-Pilot
/Radio
Operator

Radio

Hidden
Control
Yoke
(for
emergency
use)

Plasma
Cannon

Navigator's
Chair

Holographic
Navigation
Display

Cockpit

Pilot's
Chair

Steering
Yolk

Control
Console

Due to its stubby design, the C/T-3869 cargo/troop carrier has been
nicknamed "The Pug Tug." While the Pug Tug is not the fastest ship
in the fleet, it can haul a heavy payload. This craft is capable of
hauling an amazing five tons of cargo. With most of its space
allocated to troops and cargo, weapons on board are limited to four
air to air missiles and two plasma cannons. These are mounted port
and starboard, next to the cockpit.

The Pug Tug has low power anti-gravity lifts to help it hover, but
still requires standard jet lifters for take offs and landings. The
craft is powered by twin Maxadon-2000 jet engines. The Pug is
heavily armored and can take a lot of abuse. Due to the weight of
the armor, the craft is quite slow. The top speed of the Pug when
fully loaded is only Mach 1.

It was for all of these reasons that Fang Shaw acquired "The Pug
Tug" to transport the Cyborgs and Nelson on their missions.

chapter 10
Fang Shaw Revealed

AGE: 14

HOME: India

FAMILY: Mother, Father and an older brother away at university

EYE COLOR: Brown

HAIR COLOR: Black

BIRTHDAY: September 6

FAVORITE COLOR: Blue

HOBBIES: Programming VRE, Building things out of whatever he can find, fixing things. At age 7, Raj assembled a fully functioning XX-39 computer by repairing and assembling discarded parts.

PERSONALITY: Very resourceful, curious, likes to figure things out for himself.

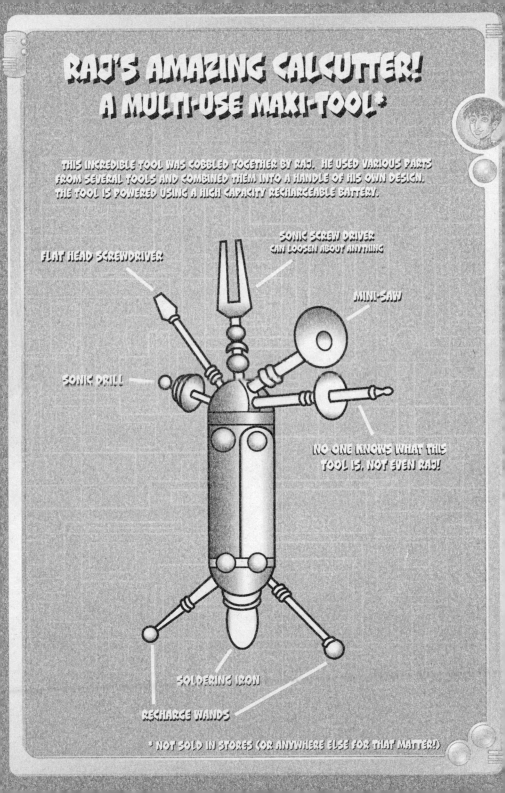

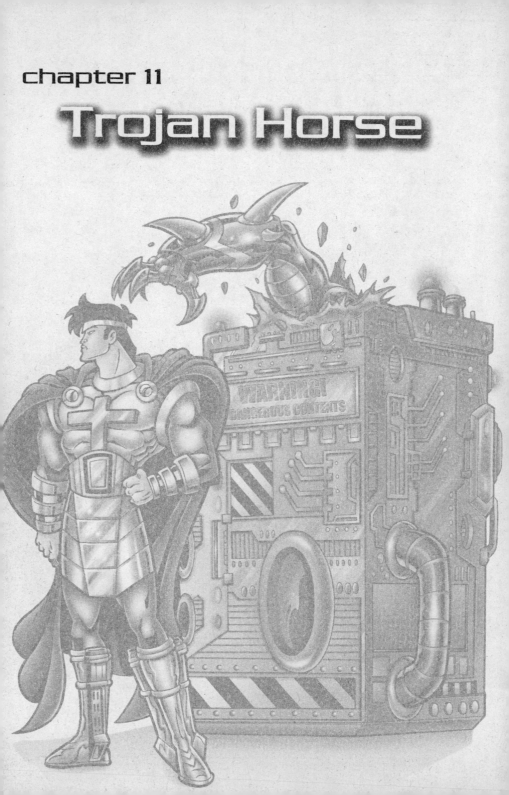

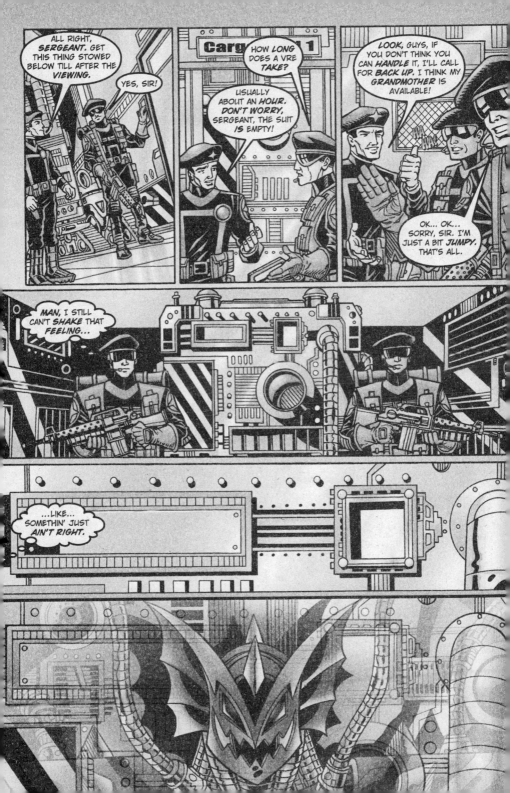

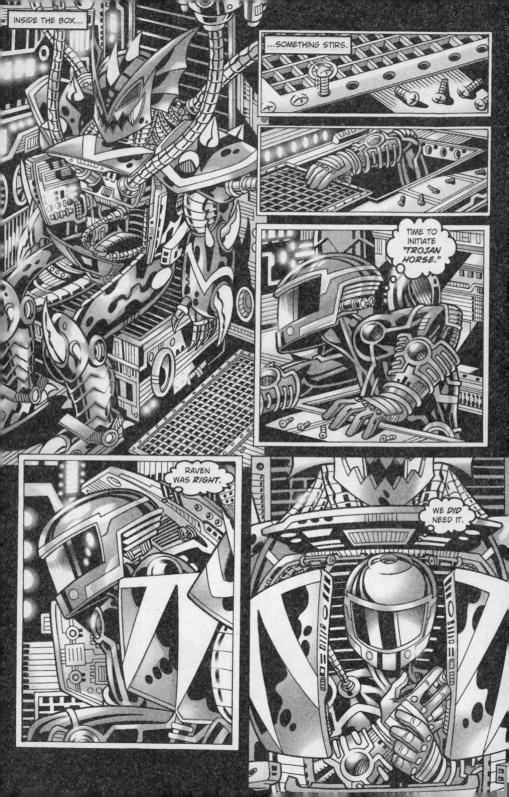

AGE: 15

HOME: New York City, USA

FAMILY: Mother

EYE COLOR: Brown

HAIR COLOR: Black

BIRTHDAY: December 27

FAVORITE FOOD: Cheeseburgers

HOBBIES: Basketball, Computers

PERSONALITY: Upbeat, competitive, street smart, honest, willing to speak his mind

TIGER CLAW

ULTRA GRID
TIGER CLAW ARMOR
NIGHT STEALTH

Soldiers never know what conditions will confront them in battle. Armor must be designed to function in a variety of situations. The Tiger Claw armor is some of the most sophisticated ever produced.

When the situation calls for stealth, this amazing armor is capable of rendering the wearer almost invisible. Tiny gel cells embedded throughout the suit change to a dark blue, almost black. This darkened look makes visual contact much more difficult and is particularly useful in night fighting.

Additionally, this amazing armor takes stealth to a new level. A special pulse activated by a low level electrical current creates a force field that blocks sensors from picking up the wearer's heat signature or vital signs.

Multi-phase visors enable the Tiger's Claw to see clearly in all conditions. Night visions, heat sensor vision and infrared "no light" vision phases ensure that these soldiers will never be left in the dark.

TROJAN

For centuries the story of the Trojan Horse was thought to be myth, but in 1871 the lost city of Troy was discovered, giving the story historical merit. It contends that the Greeks were in a long futile battle against the city of Troy. Some believe the war was over the control of a water passage; others say it was over a beautiful woman named Helen. In either case, the Greeks decided on a new approach. They built a huge, hollow wooden horse and left it outside the city gates. The people of Troy believed the Greeks had finally given up and left them a peace offering. They brought the horse into the city, and while the people of Troy slept, the Greek soldiers hiding inside the horse slipped out and opened the city gates. The Greek army entered the city and crushed their enemies.

This ploy inspired Raven and Fang Shaw's back-up plan, Trojan Horse. Having Fang Shaw accompany the suit, should it ever fall into Alliance hands, would help to secure its return. The plan included Fang Shaw wreaking havoc on the Alliance military wherever they took it... the Chameleon P-1 was the best case scenario. The Diviner was ecstatic as he thought Mark Chen would finally die at the hand of one of Mark's own family members.

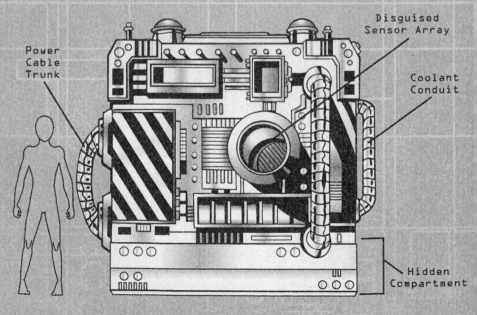

Power
Cable
Trunk

Disguised
Sensor Array

Coolant
Conduit

Hidden
Compartment

HORSE

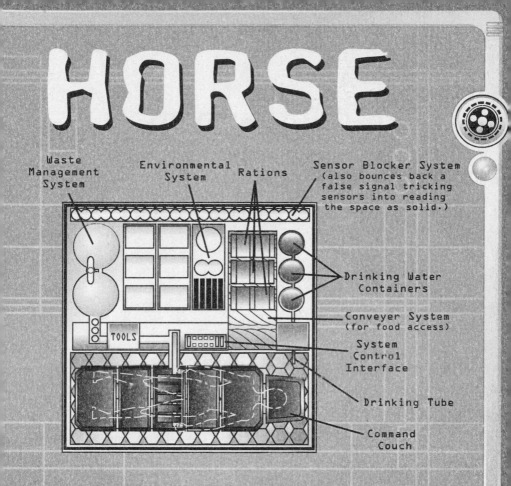

Waste
Management
System

Environmental
System

Rations

Sensor Blocker System
(also bounces back a
false signal tricking
sensors into reading
the space as solid.)

Drinking Water
Containers

Conveyer System
(for food access)

System
Control
Interface

Drinking Tube

Command
Couch

TOOLS

The contingency plan allowed Fang Shaw to hide in a compartment beneath the suit undetected. The box is normally used to store and recharge the suit. Therefore, it goes wherever Fang Shaw goes. It was at Dr. Raven's secret compound when Mark showed up unexpectedly. Fang Shaw entered the box and waited. The Alliance unknowingly took this "Trojan Horse" directly to Fang Shaw's target.

To help the hidden Fang Shaw escape with the suit, the box and suit are loaded with special technology. At the press of a button, "knock out" gas takes out anyone within a thirty-foot radius. "Lock" codes are in place to prevent the removal of the suit from the case. Concealed cameras on the box allow viewing of surroundings on an interior screen. Within the suit and box are sensor shields that block heat signatures and vital signs. The bottom compartment sends out a false signature, so when it is scanned or probed, it reads as if it is solid.

IVAN

AGE: 14

HOME: Russia

FAMILY: Mother, Father,
One older brother

EYE COLOR: Blue

HAIR COLOR: Blond

BIRTHDAY: November 15

FAVORITE FOOD: Pizza

HOBBIES: Watching Virtual-vision,
Computer Games

PERSONALITY: A loner, keeps to
himself, has had trouble
getting along with
the crew.

POWERMARK HAS FINALLY DISCOVERED THE MYSTERY OF FANG
SHAW'S IDENTITY. A CHAPTER IN HIS LIFE CLOSES, YET ANOTHER
OPENS. HE IS ABOUT TO LEARN THAT THE FORCES AGAINST HIM
ARE BOTH SINISTER AND DETERMINED. WHO ARE THEY? WHY DO
THEY PLOT AGAINST HIM? FIND OUT THE ANSWER TO THESE
QUESTIONS AS SERIES II OF POWERMARK UNFOLDS.

FROM THE AUTHOR..

DEAR READERS,

IT HAS BEEN AN INCREDIBLE PRIVILEGE TO BRING THE STORY OF
POWERMARK TO YOU EACH MONTH. I WANT YOU TO KNOW THAT I
HAVE ONLY BEGUN TO TELL HIS STORY. POWERMARK AND HIS
FRIENDS TAKE ON NEW, EVEN MORE EXCITING CHALLENGES LIKE:
WHAT HAPPENS TO THE CREW?
WILL POWERMARK EVER SEE THEM AGAIN?
WILL POWERMARK FIND ANDREW?
CAN HE PERSUADE HIM TO LEAVE LEVIATHIAN?
WHAT HAPPENS TO TRINA?
WILL SHE ROT IN PRISON?
WILL THE DIVINER BE BROUGHT TO JUSTICE?
WHAT HAPPENS TO TRINA?
WILL SHE ROT IN PRISON?
WILL THE DIVINER BE BROUGHT TO JUSTICE?
WHAT HAPPENS TO DR. RAVEN?
WILL VAPYR'S PLAN SUCCEED?
WILL JADE'S OBVIOUS FEELINGS FOR POWERMARK EVER BE
ACKNOWLEDGED?

SERIES II OPENS WITH A NEW CONQUEST UNFOLDING FOR
LEVIATHAN. OPERATION ASCENT, LEVIATHAN'S ATTEMPT TO
CONQUER MARS, IS IN FULL FORCE. BATTLES RAGE AS
CONSPIRACIES ARE PLOTTED. VILLAINS AND HEROES GO HEAD
TO HEAD. GOOD VERSUS EVIL. RIGHT VERSUS WRONG. WHICH
WILL TRIUMPH? POWERMARK VERSUS THE DIVINER. WHO
WILL EMERG THE VICTOR?
KEEP READING...

STEVE BENINTENDI
CREATOR/WRITER
POWERMARK COMICS